MW00975768

Just Ask Mom

Just Ask Mom

by Jean B. Boyce

Illustrated by Bil Keane

Creator of "The Family Circus"

International Standard Book Number
1-56684-190-9

Library of Congress Catalog Card Number
96-96166

Printed in the United States of America

Distributed by

Publishers Distribution Center Inc.
805 West 1700 South
Salt Lake City, UT 84104

Just Ask Mom

NOTHING LIKE HOME

THAT'S HOME

Home is where the lawn grows fast,
Pencils hide and toys don't last.
Home is where we pile the bills,
Talk to plants and cope with spills.
It's where the kids escape from view
The moment Mom has work to do!

ALL THAT GLITTERS . . .

Our children brighten up our home
At morning, noon, and night;
And one good reason has to be—
They leave on every light!

BIG ORDER

Our four-year-old's prayer
Was profound and precise:
"Make the bad people good,
And the good people nice."

RIGHTLY SO!

The weeks that lead to Christmas day
Can level parenthood.
But why are kids exhausted, too?
They're tired from being good!

WAYS AND MEANS

We buy a brand-new boat,
A house with all the trappings,
And then to balance things—
We reuse Christmas wrappings.

HOLIDAY HURRAH!

When he hangs up his stocking
    His mother will cheer;
It's the first bit of clothing
    He has hung up all year!

OUTDONE

Who's doing the work in our household?
Is everyone doing a share?
I find when I'm doing the dishes–
My daughter is doing her hair!

DIMINISHING RETURNS

They say that two times two is four,
And that makes sense to me;
Till socks are counted in the wash,
Then two times two is three!

FROM TOTS TO TEENS

HOME FRONT FANS

The tots say, "Yeah! Dad's home!"
They're glad, for he's their star;
The teens say, "Yeah! Dad's home–
Now we can use the car!"

RULE THE ROOST

From the day she was born
Till she entered school,
We learned all about
Minority rule.

GROWING PAINS

When a mother delivers her child
She hasn't quite earned her star—
She'll have to deliver the child
Many more years—by car!

TODAY'S VERSION

There was a young woman
Who lived in her car;
She chauffeured her children
Both nearby and far.

One day after sundown
Her youngest son said:
"You've run out of gas, Mom,
Who will drive us to bed?"

CUB SCOUT SKIT

Cub Scouts don't like to practice!
They're wiggly at this age–
First swinging on the curtains
Then leaping off the stage!

Then comes the proud performance
Their show is worth it all–
They want to form a road tour,
Or rent the City Hall!

SEMI PRECIOUS

Though mother's "little jewels"
Bring happiness and pleasure,
    On endless rainy days–
They're not her greatest treasure.

RIDING HIGH

"Look, Mom–no hands!"
(No sense–good grief!)
Next time I looked–
He had no teeth!

RATE OF EXCHANGE

Our son leaves clothes at school–
His sweater, boots, and mittens,
But brings a <u>few</u> things home,
Like measles, colds, and kittens.

PLAYERS CHOICE

Our baseball boy sits absently,
While plunking each piano key;
For any player knows
As ball or music goes–
The bench is not the place
He wants to be!

HANGUPS

It's hard to let
My teenage child
Go away to school;
But when she's gone
At least the phone–
Will have a chance to cool.

SLOW PROGRESS

Communication seems routine
To those who use a fax machine.
    Exchange we find
    With all mankind–
Except our son who turned 15!

HERE WE GO!

How come our son is jubilant,
And <u>we</u> are so distressed?
Because our six-foot baby boy
Just passed his driver's test!

SPINNING HIS WHEELS

Our teen dreams of a Ferrari,
But hopefully that will pass,
Meanwhile he's scrounging for money,
Just to buy a tank of gas.

HERE AND THERE

INFLATION VACATION

Our week in New York
Was both good and bad.
It broadened the kids–
And flattened their dad!

TEENAGE TACTICS

Could she hit a parked car
Just two households away,
Driving ten miles an hour
In the clear light of day?

We could not understand,
For we lacked some details,
Then our daughter confessed–
She was filing her nails!

WEIGHING THE ODDS

Those diet programs cost a lot!
Some may be good and some may not,
But either way–the plan is plain:
For me to lose and them to gain!

PENNY-WISE POUND FOOLISH

In spite of feeling stuffed
And wanting to be thinner,
I can't resist dessert,
If paid for—with the dinner!

COMMON BOND

I’ve never met that Mrs. B,
And yet, she’s so well-known to me.
She’s not my type, I must admit,
I’m fly-by-night and she’s true grit.

I have two cats–she has no pet,
Her mate’s retired and mine’s a vet.
She’s organized, from what I hear,
Her drawers are neat. And mine?–
    Oh, dear!

She dotes on bridge–I’d rather swim,
Yet I am plump and she is trim.
So where’s the "bond" of which I speak?
A cleaning lady shared each week.

GETTING CARRIED AWAY

Are cleaning women scarce these days?
It's true—but it's confusing;
It's not that they're tied up with work,
They've merely gone world cruising!

KEEPING PACE

We didn't need a car,
We liked the good old blue one;
But attitudes soon change—
When the neighbors buy a new one.

FOR WHAT IT'S WORTH

If social invitations count,
At times I may be slighted;
Although I wouldn't want to go,
I'd like to be invited.

HEADS OR TAILS

Although my new hairdresser
Doesn't have a lot of flair,
She's such a pro at gossip—
It's enough to curl my hair!

GOOD TIMING

The special art
Of punctuality—
Is guessing just how late
The other folks will be.

THAT FITS

My husband waits for me
(Too often—I suppose),
He claims I've got to be—
The latest thing in clothes!

WHAT'S THE RUSH?

When guests linger on
And you wish them gone,
Don't offer them rides–
Just mention your slides.

TOP OF THE LINE

The fashion world is baffling!
    The styles are so dramatic,
We can't decide if clothes have come
    From Paris—or the attic!

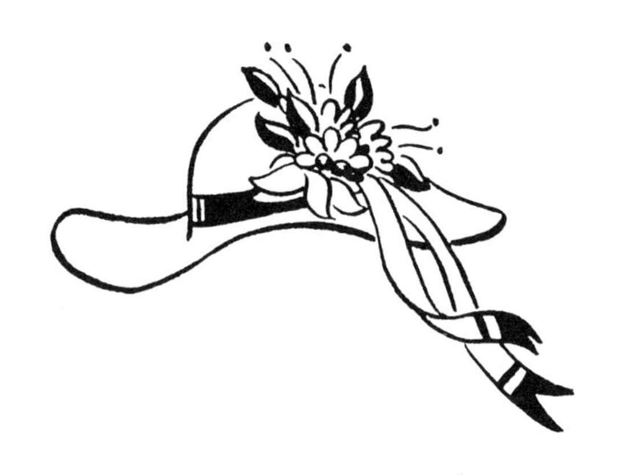

OUT OF THIS WORLD

The mystery we'll never know
Is not the way the atoms flow—
But where do combs and pencils go?

BUY BUY BUDGET

At super sales some shoppers
  Get so frantic they are funny;
They end up broke from bargains
  Designed to save them money.

SEASON'S GREETINGS

"Merry Christmas!" fills the air,
  As the holiday spirit burns,
But when it's over–merchants brace
  For "Many Happy Returns."

MEMOS ON MATES

HOLIDAY HASSLE

In our Christmas card picture
We look happy (of course)
But the trauma in process
Nearly caused a divorce.

OPEN AND SHUT CASE

It's hard to be a lawyer's wife
When arguments begin—
Though you be right and he be wrong
You still will never win!

SHORTCHANGED

He hoped she'd never change.
She hoped, somehow, he would—
But marriage may not work
Quite like we think it should.

WINNING POINT

The night you want to see a play—
Your husband says he's home to stay;
But that can change, if you suggest
You'll need his help to sand the
chest.

THE PASSWORD

Though marriage can't be perfect,
She keeps it free from stress;
Her husband gets the last word—
Provided he says, "Yes."

HIS AND HER SPORTS

At games, most men watch every play,
At least they'll know the score;
Some girls may not—and yet they'll know
What everybody wore!

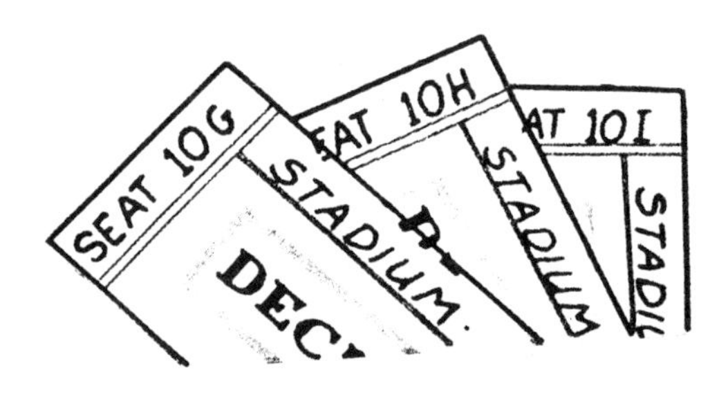

GOOD AS NEW

Old friends are great!
They're the best, I suppose,
But new friends—at least
Haven't heard all your jokes
Or seen all your clothes!

MOMENT OF TRUTH

Since "pretty is as pretty does,"
I know the reason why,
My mate thinks I'm a beauty–when
I'm making lemon pie.

HOW'S THAT AGAIN?

A wife should praise her husband
And thereby make his day:
"You're really doing well, dear,
Despite what people say!"

HEAR THIS

Is it just coincidence,
Or something else more shocking,
That the husbands who go deaf—
Have wives who don't stop talking?

LONG SINCE

He used to bring long roses,
  But comes home now instead,
With something long, but useful—
  A plunger or French bread.

JUST BETWEEN US

OUT OF FOCUS

When bringing up our first one
We reached the "picture age,"
With snaps and slides and movies
Of each exciting stage.

With every child that followed
Our cameras had less use,
Till shots were most infrequent
Of little Miss Caboose.

One day she made a comment
That shattered my aplomb—
She summed it up by saying:
"Was I adopted, Mom?"

RELATIVELY SPEAKING

It's *great* to be the youngest child,
When parents act more lax and mild.
The older kids can do the chores,
While I am free to play outdoors.

It's *tough* to be the youngest child,
The constant teasing drives me wild,
Too many kids to share the beds,
And hand-me-downs almost in shreds!

MAY POLL

Of all the months we have each year,
The one most folks enjoy is May—
With income tax behind—at last,
And Christmas seven months away!

BEST LAID SCHEMES

To stop forgetting names
Became his resolution.
A way to help recall
Seemed like a good solution.
Except it crossed him up—
(He really pulled a sizzler),
Miss Swindle was her name—
He struck out with Miss Chiseler!

LAUGHING MATTER

Embarrassing moments
Are funny jokes,
Provided they happen
To other folks.

ON THE TRIGGER

While most of us keep busy,
Some people never shirk–
They hear an idle rumor
And put it right to work!

PENNYWORTH

Inflation doesn't always
    Raise the price–
A penny for your thoughts
    May still suffice.

JUST WHAT I WANTED

I don't like to open a gift,
The reason is foolish—but true;
I fear I won't like what's inside
And have to pretend that I do!

YESTERDAY'S NEWS

Her secrets aren't much fun!
She says: "Don't breathe a word."
But when I tell someone,
Already—they have heard!

CHRISTMAS GREENS

Although we like the mistletoe,
And the fresh-cut Christmas tree,
The U.S. mint supplies the green
That most of us like to see.

CHEERY WEARY

Once Christmas was a single day,
Then things got out of reason;
From Halloween to Valentine
Is now the Christmas season!

THE SENIOR SLANT

GRANDPARENTING

My grandsons bring me lots of joy,
  In fact–it sets my heart aglow,
To see the little angels come–
  And watch the little devils go!

DOWN THE LINE

As a woman grows older,
Her judgment gets better;
She cares how her shoes fit,
Instead of her sweater!

NO LEEWAY

It's tough to have my last child gone
I might as well admit it;
Now anything that's out of whack–
My husband knows I did it.

ON TRACK

Grandmas today don't baby sit,
They don't crochet–they do stay fit.
Old soldiers fade, but that's okay,
Grandmas don't die–they jog away!

WELL ROUNDED

Why can't I retain
The things that I learn
And hopefully be more elite?
Instead–it's quite plain
How well I retain
The bulk of the things
    that I eat!

WHAT A WAIST

He still retains his youthful weight,
    It changes very little.
The only problem seems to be–
    It's shifted to the middle!

MISS CONFIDENCE

"I'll fix your toy," her grandpa said,
"There's surely nothing to it."
"How can you?" snapped our 5-year-old,
"When even I can't do it!"

DON'T CALL ME

The time when youth departs
And middle age comes through,
Is when you hear the phone–
And hope it's not for you!

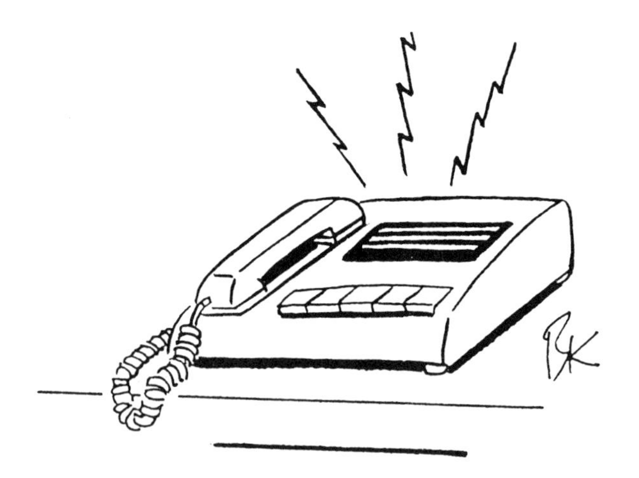

ON THE HOUSE

By this time in life
We know what to expect–
When youth calls to age
It is always collect!

LAYS 'EM LOW

Recovery rooms are used
For patients who are ill,
Including folks in shock—
Who just received their bill!

FOR A CHANGE

Most wives who cook will tell you
Without much hesitation—
Their favorite thing for dinner
Is one good reservation!

HEAD START

Great-grandpa in his eighties
Was one to plan ahead;
He phoned at five one morning
And got us out of bed.

He had an old folks meeting
And so he'd called to say:
"I'll need some transportation,
It's one week from today!"

ACROSS THE FENCE

"The tales folks tell about me
Are false," says Neighbor Wood,
"Don't listen to their chatter–
I'm really not that good."

NOTHING LIKE IT

Experience is great,
  It tells you when
You've made the same
  Mistake again.

THAT'S LIFE

From ABC to Ph.D
Takes 30 years or so,
Then FHA and PTA
May be the route we go.
So PDQ the years go by,
From IOU's we're free
  Then Dads retire
  But Mothers don't—
They still are on KP!

ACKNOWLEDGMENTS

The verses in this book first appeared in the following publications (reprinted with permission):

FAMILY CIRCLE - Out Of This World

FAMILY WEEKLY (Quips & Quotes) - Penny-Wise Pound Foolish

GOOD HOUSEKEEPING - No Leeway, Holiday Hurrah! All That Glitters . . .

GRIT (Talelights) - Relatively Speaking, Player's Choice, Grandparenting, Nothing Like It, Christmas Greens, Semi-Precious, Season's Greetings, Today's Version

McCALL'S - What's the Rush?, Don't Call Me, On the House

THE NEW YORK TIMES (Metropolitan Diary) Ways and Means

QUOTE (Quotable Speakers) - Well Rounded

SATURDAY EVENING POST (Post Scripts) - Down the Line, Holiday Hassle, Outdone, That's Home

UTAH SINGS, Volume Seven (Utah State Poetry Society) - Top Of The Line, May Poll, His and Her Sports

THE WALL STREET JOURNAL (Pepper and Salt) For What It's Worth, That's Life